Ned, Fred & Friend

A Bedtime Story

by
Dr. Ron Madison

Illustrations by
David Covolo

ISBN 1-887206-03-5 Printed in the U.S.A.

Can you read with me?
It's easy as pie.
I'll give you some hints.
So give it a try.

When you see *NED*,
Just say *"NED"*

When you see *FRED*
Just say *"FRED"*

When you see *FRIEND*
Just say *"FRIEND"*

And don't forget
It's easy to rhyme
The words that come
At the end of each line.

Dr Ron

NED CHASED FRED in a friendly race

Deep in the woods to their special place

Where they would find peace and grace

And often enjoy a friendly embrace.

But FRED stopped short, took a Boogle pose.

There was something strange in front of his nose.

NED crept forward on the tip of his toes,

When suddenly the "thing" stirred and rose.

And then NED realized he had nothing to fear.

It was a little brown bear, that much was clear,

But it was hungry and cold, its eye held a tear.

It was lost, for sure, and in much need of cheer.

"Come home with us," NED said to the bear,

"Where it's warm and nice and we've food there."

To the bear that sounded exceedingly fair,

And the bear joined forever our friendly pair.

Suddenly NED knew what it was like to be

The giver of love, like in a family.

To help someone else helped NED, you see,

And the inseparable two became the inseparable three.

The bear they called "FRIEND," and ever since then,

You never saw three close as NED, FRED and FRIEND.

And snug in their bed at every day's end,

They would dream of tomorrow

And the joys they would spend.